A Christmas Story for Rachel Rabbit

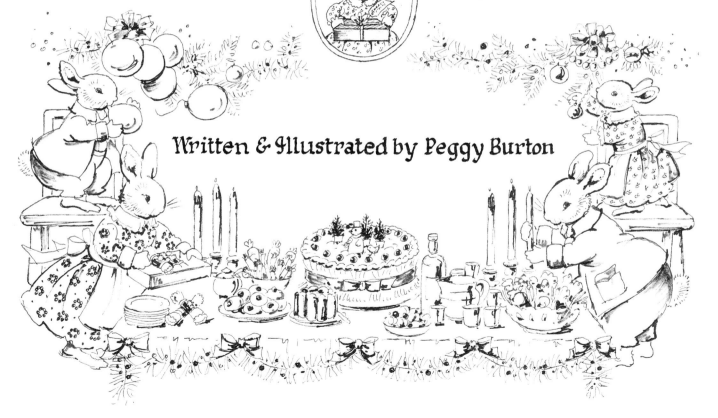

Written & Illustrated by Peggy Burton

© THE MEDICI SOCIETY LTD · LONDON · 1990.   Printed in England.   ISBN 0 85503 157 3

Mrs Rabbit had made a lovely Christmas cake with currants, nuts, cherries, honey and other good things in it and she was now busy covering it with snowy white icing and decorating it to look beautiful.

Her two young ones, Roddy and Rachel watched excitedly. 'This is a very special cake,' said Mrs Rabbit, 'because Uncle Joe and Aunt Jane and their two young ones, Peter and Patsy, are coming to spend Christmas with us.'

'Where do they live?' asked Rachel. 'Come over here and I'll show you,' said her mother. She picked up Rachel in her arms and pointed out of the window. 'You see that clump of trees at the top of the hill across the valley, that's Hill Top Wood and that's where they live.' 'Goody!' said Rachel, 'That will be fun.'

When Roddy and Rachel awoke next morning there had been a further fall of snow which had covered the entrance to their burrow. 'Now you two,' said Pa Rabbit, 'You'll have to help me clear a pathway for our visitors.'

All the family worked hard; they made a bigger entrance and cleared the snow from the path and front door. It was decided that Aunt Jane would have the spare room and that the little room would be cleared so that all the young ones could be together.

'I'll take some of our toys and games in there,' said Roddy. 'But first we must move the beds and furniture around and get the room ready,' said Mrs Rabbit.

Meanwhile, up at Hill Top Wood, Uncle Joe, Aunt Jane, Peter and Patsy were getting ready for their journey to the Rabbit Family on the other side of the valley.

They wrapped up all the presents that they would be giving each other and the ones they would be taking for the Rabbit Family.

Then Uncle Joe went to get the sledge and made sure it was in a good enough state to stand the journey down the steep part of the hill.

They packed things they would need to have with them into a case and put all the presents into a big box. Then they put everything onto the sledge, so that they would be ready to start on their journey early next morning.

Next morning they set off through the snow which was sparkling in the sunlight. Uncle Joe pulled the sledge while the others walked alongside. When they came to the slopes Uncle Joe settled Peter and Patsy on the sledge and showed Peter how to hold the rope so that all would go well.

Peter and Patsy were having fun as the sledge went steadily down the hill. They were singing and bouncing about when suddenly, as they passed near Maurice Mouse's house, the sledge hit a log hidden by the snow. The sledge wobbled; the case fell off and tripped up Uncle Joe; the box tipped over spilling presents – and the sledge careered down the hill until it stopped with a bump at a big bush.

Pigeon Postman flying overhead came down to help and said that he was on the way to the Rabbit house and he would tell Mrs Rabbit that they had been delayed.

9

Roddy and Rachel kept running to the window to see if their visitors were coming.

Suddenly Roddy shouted 'Pigeon Postman is coming here!' 'Good morning!' said Postman, 'I have a message from your visitors that they have had a mishap on the way; they spilled parcels on the hill and it will make them a bit late. Also, I have some letters and cards for you.'

Mrs Rabbit thanked Postman for bringing the message and wished him a Happy Christmas. Then he flew off to continue his deliveries.

Very soon afterwards the visitors arrived. They were all pleased to see each other and there was much fun and laughter when Peter and Patsy told Roddy and Rachel about their adventure on the hill. Meanwhile the grown-ups chatted and caught up with the news.

After lunch, Mrs Rabbit said to Aunt Jane, 'As it's Christmas Eve, will you come with me and the young ones to take presents to some of our lonely friends living near here, while the men decorate the Christmas tree?' 'I'd like that,' said Aunt Jane.

Roddy, Peter and Patsy went to visit dear Doctor Drake who cared for everbody when they were unwell, but had nobody to care for him. He thanked them for coming. Then he smiled and said, 'Don't eat too much Christmas pudding or I'll have to give you some medicine!' They all laughed and went on their way.

Mrs Rabbit, Rachel and Aunt Jane, had gone to visit Harriet Hedgehog who lived by herself. It was lovely to see how pleased she and all their friends were to have a chat, and, on the way home, Rachel gave her mother a big kiss for all her kindness.

Mr and Mrs Rabbit were having a Christmas Eve supper party for their guests. The room was gaily decorated with holly and paper chains and the table was laid with lovely things to eat.

After supper, which they all enjoyed very much, they played party games including 'Blind Man's Buff' and 'Musical Chairs'. They walked around the row of chairs while Roddy Rabbit beat on his drum, and when he stopped suddenly they all tumbled over each other to sit on one of the chairs.

Then Uncle Joe played on his recorder while they all sang Christmas Carols.

When the party was over, the four young ones hung up their stockings and went to bed eagerly looking forward to Christmas Day.

17

While the Rabbits' party was going on, Maurice Mouse went outside with lantern and basket to get more logs for his fire.

He lived on the side of the hill near Hill Top Wood and kept his pile of logs near the house. He thought he'd better take some more inside, before they were all covered with snow.

As he put a few in the basket, his lantern shone on what looked like a brightly coloured parcel. He took it inside to look at it properly and found that it was a Christmas present with a tag, which read, 'To Rachel, with love from Uncle Joe and Aunt Jane'.

'Oh, dear,' thought Maurice, 'I wonder who that belongs to, 'I'd better ask Pigeon Postman in the morning. I expect he will know and I wonder how it got amongst my logs.'

On Christmas morning the young rabbits were awake early to see what Santa had brought for them. Mrs Rabbit and Aunt Jane were preparing lunch and Mr Rabbit and Uncle Joe were putting the presents round the Christmas tree.

The four young ones spent the morning playing in the snow which made them very hungry. They all had lunch and when it was over Mr Rabbit said, 'I think it's time we had our presents.' 'Yes!' cried the youngsters as they ran to the tree.

Mr and Mrs Rabbit gave out all the presents they had for everybody and soon there was a pile of paper as they all looked to see what they had been given.

But when Uncle Joe and Aunt Jane had finished giving out the presents from Hill Top Wood, they were sad to find that there wasn't one for Rachel.

'I'm sure I packed it,' said Aunt Jane. 'Perhaps it was lost on the hill,' said Patsy. 'I'm sure you are right,' said Uncle Joe.

They were all feeling very downhearted when, who did they see flying towards them but Pigeon Postman – with a parcel held in his beak by the string!

He landed near them and said, 'Maurice Mouse found this amongst his pile of logs but didn't know who it belonged to. So when he showed it to me I thought I'd better get it to you very quickly.' 'Oh! You clever Postman!' said Mrs Rabbit.

Everybody was smiling again as Rachel opened her present to discover a little red velvet jacket with white fur on it. 'Oh! It's lovely!' said Rachel as she put it on. 'Thank you Aunt Jane and Uncle Joe, and thank you Mr Postman.'

They invited Pigeon Postman in for a piece of Christmas cake and a cup of tea, and when it was time for him to go, Rachel, still in her little red jacket, went outside and waved to him until he was out of sight, saying to herself, 'What a dear kind Pigeon he is,' and 'How we have enjoyed our Christmas!'.